Ugly Pie

Lisa Wheeler   Illustrated by Heather Solomon

HARCOURT CHILDREN'S BOOKS
Houghton Mifflin Harcourt
Boston • New York • 2010

Harcourt Children's Books is an imprint of Houghton Mifflin Harcourt Publishing Company.
www.hmhbooks.com

The paintings in this book were done in watercolor, acrylic, and collage on paper.
The text type was set in Chauncy Decaf.
The display type was set in Sodom.

Library of Congress Cataloging-in-Publication Data
Wheeler, Lisa, 1963–
Ugly Pie/Lisa Wheeler; illustrated by Heather Solomon.
p. cm.
Summary: After baking a scrumptious Ugly Pie, made from ingredients donated by
his neighbors, Ol' Bear invites everyone over for a slice. Includes pie recipe.
[1. Pies—Fiction. 2. Bears—Fiction.] I. Solomon, Heather, ill. II. Title.
PZ7.W5657Ug   2010
[E]—dc22   2008004535
ISBN 978-0-15-216754-7

Printed in China
LEO 10 9 8 7 6 5 4 3 2 1
4500213855

For Carol Haroulakis and Christine Shaw,
who baked the first Ugly Pie,
and for Dennis, who ate it
—L.W.

For Aden, my son—H.S.

O l' Bear woke up one morning with a hankerin' for pie. Not just any pie. **Ugly Pie.**

But the only ugly thing he had in his kitchen was some gooey sweet molasses. It tasted just fine, but it wasn't what Ol' Bear was itchin' for.

So with a heap of hope and a hitch of his britches, Ol' Bear went off in search of Ugly Pie.

As he walked along, he sang a song.

"Sweet molasses, my-oh-my. I'm itchin' for some Ugly Pie!"

When Ol' Bear came to Grampa Grizzle's house, he paused for a little sniff. "My-oh-my-oh-my! Do I smell Ugly Pie?"

Grampa Grizzle opened his front door. "I don't have no Ugly Pie, but you should give my pie a try—

my pleasin' pumpkin pie!"

"That sure is one plump and pleasin' pie,"
Ol' Bear said. "But I'm just itchin'—
truly itchin'—for some **Ugly Pie**."

"The only ugly things I got in my kitchen are these wrinkled red raisins," said Grampa. "But they're yours if you want 'em."

Ol' Bear thanked Grampa Grizzle, popped a raisin into his mouth, and continued on his way.

As he walked along, he sang a song.

"Ruby raisins—not too dry,
sweet molasses, my-oh-my!
But I'm still itchin',
sniffin', wishin'
for some **Ugly Pie!**"

Soon Ol' Bear stood in front of the home
of Ma Hickory and her two cubs, Snip and Snarl.
His nose gave a little twitch. "My-oh-my-oh-my!
Do I smell Ugly Pie?"

Snip and Snarl opened the door. "We don't have no
Ugly Pie, but you should give *Ma's* pie a try—

her righteous rhubarb pie!"

"That sure is one righteous pie," Ol' Bear said. "But I'm just itchin'—*truly itchin'*— for some **Ugly Pie**."

"The only ugly things I got in my kitchen are these sour green apples," said Ma Hickory. "But they're yours if you want 'em."

Ol' Bear thanked the Hickory family, dropped the
apples into his pockets, and hurried on his way.

As he walked along, he sang a song.

"Got the apples of my eye,
Ruby raisins—not too dry,
sweet molasses, my-oh-my!
But I'm still itchin',
twitchin', wishin'
for some **Ugly Pie!**"

In a short while, Ol' Bear came to the home of
Sweet Cicely. He sighed a little sigh. "My-oh-my-oh-my!
Do I smell Ugly Pie?"

Sweet Cicely opened the door. "I don't have no
Ugly Pie, but you should give my pie a try—

my heavenly honey pie!"

"That sure is one honey of a pie," Ol' Bear said. "But I'm just itchin'—truly itchin'—for some **Ugly Pie**."

"The only ugly things I got in my kitchen are these bumpy brown walnuts," said Sweet Cicely. "But they're yours if you want 'em."

Ol' Bear thanked Sweet Cicely, slipped the
walnuts into his bag, and headed on home.

As he walked along, he sang a song.

"I got apples, raisins, too,
nuts, molasses, but I'm blue.
Nothin' else will satisfy
my cravin' for some Ugly Pie."

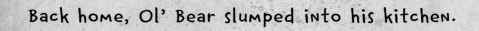

Back home, Ol' Bear slumped into his kitchen.

He unpacked the wrinkled red raisins.
"Those sure are some **ugly** raisins."

He unpacked the sour green apples.
"These are the **ugliest** apples I've ever seen."

He unpacked the bumpy brown walnuts.
"And what am I supposed to do with such **ugly** walnuts?"

Ol' Bear scratched his head. "Walnuts—wait a minute!"

"Ugly apples,
raisins, too,
sweet molasses, nuts—
WA-HOO!

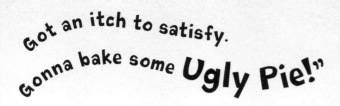

Got an itch to satisfy.
Gonna bake some **Ugly Pie!**"

Then Ol' Bear commenced
to a-choppin'
and a-mixin'

and a-stirrin'
and a-fixin'

and a-rollin'
and a-makin'
**an Ugly Pie just
fit for bakin'!**

And quicker than you can say Granny Smith, Ol' Bear's den filled with a taste-bud-temptin' aroma.

His nose itched.
His toes twitched.

His heart sang.
His doorbell rang!

DING-DONG!

Ol' Bear opened his door, and there stood Grampa Grizzle,
Ma Hickory, Snip, Snarl, and Sweet Cicely!
"My-oh-my-oh-my!" they called. "Do we smell pie?"

"Not just any pie," Ol' Bear said. **"UGLY PIE!** And I'm
just itchin'—*truly itchin'*—

for a passel of neighbors to share it with!"

"Apples, nuts, red raisins, too!
We love Ugly Pie—we do!

We're so glad that we could try

Ol' Bear's scrumptious—

truly wondrous—beautiful Ugly Pie!

WA-HOO!"

If you've been itchin' for some Ugly Pie, today is your lucky day! Here's Ol' Bear's recipe, handed down from bear to bear for generations.

Remember, cubs in the kitchen should always have a big bear around while cookin'.

RECIPE FOR UGLY PIE

Ugly Crust

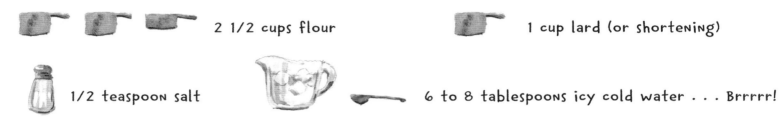

2 1/2 cups flour   1 cup lard (or shortening)

1/2 teaspoon salt   6 to 8 tablespoons icy cold water . . . Brrrrr!

First, mix together the flour and salt. Then, using a fork, cut little chunks of that ugly lard into your flour until you get what looks like itty-bitty pea-sized balls. Set aside half this mixture in another bowl for later. Next, sprinkle 1 tablespoon of icy cold water over those pea-sized balls. Gently toss it with a fork. Repeat until your flour mixture forms an ugly ball of dough.

Spread a little bit of flour out on a flat surface (like your kitchen counter). Pat that ball of ugly dough down like you mean business. Then roll it with a rolling pin until it becomes a flat, ugly crust. It doesn't matter if it looks nice and round and pretty. This is Ugly Pie! Place in 9" deep-dish pie plate.

Ugly Filling

6 cups peeled, sliced Granny Smith apples   1/4 cup molasses
1 teaspoon lemon juice

In a large bowl, toss apple slices with lemon juice. Then mix in molasses until apples are completely coated with ugly brown goo. Set aside.

5 tablespoons flour   1/2 cup white sugar
1 teaspoon cinnamon   3/4 cup brown sugar
1/2 teaspoon nutmeg

In a medium-sized bowl, mix the dry ingredients listed above. Add to the ugly apple mixture until everything is nice 'n' moist.

3/4 cup red raisins (cran-raisins work great!)

1/4 walnuts—chopped fine

Toss raisins and walnuts into apple mixture. Make sure all ingredients are well coated. Place into pie crust. Your pie should look fairly ugly by now.

Ugly Topping

Take the crumbly flour mixture you set aside earlier. Sprinkle over the top of the pie.

Cover pie with an aluminum-foil tent to prevent overbrowning. Bake at 400 degrees for 40 minutes. Remove foil and bake another 20 minutes.

When your pie is done, you will have the most delicious, most beautiful **Ugly Pie** you ever saw.

My-oh-my-oh-my!